Diary of a Roblox Noob: The Riddle-Man of Roblox Bloxburg!

By Robloxia Kid

Great Roblox The Riddle-Man of Roblox Bloxburg!

FREE
INSTANT DOWNLOAD

Unofficial Roblox Story

DIARY OF
A ROBLOX NOOB

JAILBREAK

freebie.robloxiakid.com

Contents

Chapter One

The Dogs of Paradise.

Hi kiddies, and everyone else! My name's Noob, and I'm a Roblox adventurer. What do I do? Well, I wander all around the different Roblox servers looking for action and adventure. You could say that I'm some kind of wandering soul whose only purpose in life is to look for adventure! I live life to the fullest, making the most of every opportunity and experience as it presents itself. Believe me, with so many servers in Roblox to wander to and from, I've got more than a lot of experiences to enjoy!

Is it an unusual choice of life? Of course it is, and that's why I love it so much! You see, I'm not the kind of guy who likes to lie around all day at home, or work all day in an office getting his back sore from leaning and typing over a computer. Nope, not your Noob! No way! I'm the kind of guy that likes to make the most out of every moment in life. The kind of guy who likes to live life on the edge. You could say that I'm in love with wandering and adventure. I'm kinda in a perpetual state of wanderlust.

It all sounds and cool, and in many ways yeah, it really is. I mean, who wouldn't want to wander from server to server in the wide and wonderful world of Roblox looking for adventure, eh? I've seen and experienced it all. I've survived disasters, shot down cowboys and terrorists, and even chopped wood and farmed land. Yep, I've done it all.

You would think that such a lifestyle wouldn't have its downside, but unfortunately, it does. The biggest drawback? The moolah, the greenbacks, the big bucks. The cash. The Robux. My lifestyle doesn't really pay that well. I know that sounds pretty blunt, but it's true. I think I don't even need to elaborate when I say that it can be pretty tough not making those Robux. The sting of those adventures can really be blunted without the cash to just well, keep going.

So there I was, really short on cash and wandering towards my next adventure. I'm pretty used to having a zero bank account by now. I'm always a muscle car running on fumes, so I guess I wasn't bothered too much about it. At least not as bothered as I could be. I tried to keep my money problems to myself and kept wandering. Eventually, I stumbled onto another server, and my next adventure.

I looked around and saw what could only be described as the perfect vision of modern suburbia. What do I mean? Well, for one thing, I saw rows and rows of cute and dainty little houses. The houses had those stylish and pointed roofs with perfect color schemes that matched the walls of the houses. There wasn't a splotch of paint that was out of place, and they all appeared perfect and newly painted. The lawns were perfectly manicured, and no weeds or grass was overgrown. The flowers in the little gardens beside the houses were all in bloom. I could also see some dogs that sat lazily in front of the some of the houses' porches. The pooches all appeared sleepy, full, and very content.

"This looks like paradise!" I said.

Of course, just like in any server in Roblox, I would later learn that this place was anything but paradise. After all, you can't have adventures in paradise, right? I don't know, I guess I'm kinda ranting so forget that.

Anyway, the whole place was so appealing. It was so cute, almost like the scene from a postcard so I just had to wander towards the houses.

I was smiling as I approached the place, but my smile would soon be wiped from my face. As soon as I approached the houses, the nearest dog in front of me suddenly started barking. He leapt instantly towards me, and I was actually amazed by it. Like the other dogs, he had been lazily lying on the front porch of his house. How he instantly jumped up and rushed towards me was frankly, unbelievable. It was almost like a switch had been turned on, and the family friendly pet had turned into a killing machine.

The dog made several primal sounds as it ran towards me on all-fours. I began to wonder if this was really a pet, or some kind of prehistoric wolf in disguise. For a moment, my eyes widened and I was frozen with fear. I was like a deer caught in the headlights of a car that was about to turn it into roadkill. I couldn't understand what was happening, but only for a moment. I began to run for my life.

"Yeow! Get away!"

Of course, Fido didn't listen to me. Like most persistent dogs, once he had zeroed in on me, there was no turning back. There was only one thing, and one thing only in Fido's mind, and that was to rip my head off from my neck. That was already bad enough in itself, but it was about to get a lot worse.

I looked back, and apparently the pack mentality of the other dogs had kicked in. They were all inspired by Fido's heroic example, and started chasing me down the block, as well. Before I knew it, I had several rabid dogs from paradise breathing down my neck.

"Stay away from me! I was just passing by the place! I don't want to hurt anybody!"

Somehow, I managed to keep one step away from the crazy things. Don't ask me how I managed to keep one step ahead of them. I could literally smell their doggie breaths behind my neck the whole time. I guess it was just the fear of getting mauled by a pack of dogs. After all, if all of my adventures had taught me anything, it was that the urge to stay alive was the strongest urge of all.

"Get away already!"

Remember all that hot pooch-breath that I was talking about earlier? Well, in one terrible instant, I felt them all over me. I thought that they would all pounce on me, all at once. I thought that yeah, I was doomed.

"It was a great life while it lasted, Noob. Thanks for the memories."

That was the last thought on my mind, as I slipped and fell on the pavement. I landed with a loud thud, and I closed my eyes. Yeah, I was doomed all right, and I decided to just accept my fate.

Chapter Two

Broke and in the Slammer.

I opened my eyes, and I was flat on my back. I looked up and saw the blue sky above me. There wasn't a cloud in sight, and the sun was shining down on me. I thought I saw the sun looking down on me, and smiling. I think he had big eyes and fat cheeks. I could also notice that he had a long and very pronounced lips. His lips was large and very well, kissable. His nose was also a lot bigger than I thought it would be. Mr. Sun was in a very cheerful mood and he seemed very aggeeable.

"I'm alive. I'm still alive." I said.

I had to be alive. The sun shining down on me and the sky was proof enough of that.

Slowly, I got up. I was still shaking and I managed to look around me for a better view. The dogs were all standing in front of me. They were all panting with their tongues out. It was a sure sign that they were tired from all the chasing, and were exhausted. With their tongues out, they actually looked a little funny and appeared to be smiling at me. It was like that switch was flipped again, and they were back to their cute and huggable selves. Lucky for me. Still, I wasn't fooled by them anymore. I had already seen what these crazy beasts were capable of, first-hand. What I didn't understand was, why I was still breathing. They could have taken me down, but they were docile and peaceful again.

"What just happened?" I said.

"Get up!"

The voice was gruff and quite authoritative. This guy meant business. I already knew that he was a cop before I even saw him. Someone who spoke that way just had to be a cop. My cop hunch was confirmed when I saw the police car behind him. There was a siren that started to screech and light up above the cop car.

"I already am up!"

"Oh, a wise ass eh? We don't like wise asses here at Bloxburg!"

I realized that I should not have cracked that remark. The cop pushed me towards the police car, and slammed me against the door.

"Ouch! Take it easy, already!"

"I ain't takin' it easy against an intruder like yourself, especially someone like you, who's been terrorizing the neighborhood!"

The police officer put my wrists together and slapped on a pair of cuffs. I realized that I was being arrested. No money, and a trip to the slammer? How bad could it get? I could see that my adventure here in this new server was off to a wonderful start.

"Bloxburg? This place is called Bloxburg?" I asked.

"Stop playing dummy, Riddle-Man! We've been on your tail for a long time now, but you've finally slipped up! When those dogs growled at you, we knew that we had our man!"

The cop was talking in well, riddles. He could have been speaking a foreign language for all I cared. I had no idea what he was talking about.

"Mister, I don't know what you're talking about! I'm not even sure I know where this is. I was just wandering into your town, Bloxburg, right? Once I got here, your crazy pooches all snapped and went after me! And by the way, my name's not Riddle-Man! It's Noob!"

"Cut the fake names already, Riddle-Man! Those pet pooches are sweet and loving to their owners, but mean on crooks Riddle-Man! You've avoided capture for so long, but now you finally slipped up! I guess you simply got too arrogant for your own good!"

"Come on, mister! I don't know what you're.."

Before I could even finish, the policeman hauled me into his car, and drove away. I looked behind me. Those crazy dogs got smaller and smaller, as the police car drove away. They were soon dots on the rear window, and then they finally disappeared. Yep, this was turning out to be a great adventure, so far.

Chapter Three

The First Riddle.

"Stay there, and get comfortable. You're going to be rotting in that cell for a very long time!"

I was taken to Bloxburg's police precinct, and the cop threw me in a cage. I could see the policeman from behind the bars, as he typed and did his office work. There were other policemen all around the office. It was a busy day in the police precinct, and well, he was right. I was just starting to rot in my cell.

The cell itself wasn't so bad. It was a large space, big enough for me to walk around and stretch my legs. I wasn't cramped or anything, but there was no way that I was getting out of there. I could also see the other policemen doing their daily routine, and somehow, that just made my stay a lot worse. I knew that I was innocent, and there was no reason in the world for me to be behind bars. I just didn't know how I could possibly prove that to the policeman who had arrested me.

I didn't know it then, but I wouldn't have to.

"Chief Penny, this just came in!"

Another policeman approached Chief Penny. The policeman was frantic and clearly stressed. So I was arrested by the Chief of Police in Bloxburg himself. That was really great.

"Whoa, slow down Roxy! Slow down and tell me what's.."

"Maybe I ought to just show you, Chief! Look!"

Poor Roxy was shaking as he handed the chief a simple white piece of paper. It was a note, and from where I was sitting, I had no way of reading the contents. The chief however could read it perfectly, and had already glanced it. I noticed he turned pale, and all the color left his face after he was done.

He turned to me, with a different look on his face.

"You're free to go, kid. I mean, Noob." he said.

I couldn't believe what I was hearing.

"Whoa, whoa. What are you talking about?"

The chief appeared annoyed and irritated by my confusion.

"Do I have to spell it out for you? You're free to go! Now, get out, already!"

The chief unlocked the cell door and it turned with a loud squeaky noise. He motioned with his hand to show me the way out. His hand was still holding the note that Roxy had shown him.

"I'm not going to let out a red carpet for you, Noob. If you expect an apology, you won't get it. Just get out, already! I still have real work to do!"

I still couldn't understand it, but I decided to finally take the chief on his offer.

"All right fine, fine already!"

I walked out of the cell, and I was a free man again. I had spent a grand total of twenty minutes in the cell. I was free, but I was still curious as to what was going on around here.

"What's going on, Chief? And why did you suddenly let me go? And who is the Riddle-Man, anyway?"

"For a homeless bum who wandered into our perfect little town, you've sure got a lot of questions!" the Chief barked.

"I'll answer them for you, Noob. I guess you do deserve some kind of explanation after what happened."

It was Roxy. He sure seemed a lot more friendly than the chief and I was grateful for that.

"You see, our peaceful little suburb of Bloxburg has been terrorized for awhile now, by a mysterious thief."

"A thief! So I guess this town wasn't as peaceful and

paradise-like than I thought!"

"We don't really have that many problems, but this thief has really been driving everyone nuts. He breaks into people's homes and steals a lot of their valuables."

"I don't get it, Officer Roxy. I marched into town and I didn't see a single smashed window or loose door. All the houses looked neat and perfect-like. They sure didn't look like anyone broke into them."

"Credit that to the homeowners. They just love their houses to be so neat and tidy. They'll go to any lengths to keep them shiny and almost brand-new like the day they bought them. When the thief breaks into the house, we make an investigation, but the homeowners are so concerned with keeping things neat, they always fix up the house before we even get there. Believe me, this only makes our job of catching this guy even more difficult."

It was the chief who spoke now. I could sense the frustration in his voice.

"I guess that must be tough. Don't tell me. This thief. He's the.."

"..Riddle-Man. Yeah, you guessed it right, Noob. That's what the papers call him. They gave him that nickname because he has this really annoying habit of poking fun at us by leaving riddles in the scene of his crimes." Roxy said.

"The guy fancies himself as some kind of a genius.

He thinks that he's smarter than all of us, and we can't catch him. The riddles are there to taunt and insult us. I have to admit, he's actually making us look like fools." the chief said.

"You'll have to forgive the chief for what happened earlier, Noob. We're all determined to catch the Riddle-Man. There's even been a reward posted for his capture. That's why everyone is on edge. When you just strolled into town, the chief got anxious and arrested you. On behalf of the police and the chief, I apologize." Roxy said.

The chief frowned at Roxy, and I thought I heard him growl like those dogs earlier. Roxy was taking a big risk apologizing like that. I could see that the chief was not the kind of man who could accept a mistake. He had a lot of pride being the police chief of a clean and neat town like Bloxburg, and I could see that the Riddle-Man was taking advantage of this pride. It was easy to mess someone up like that, and the chief's pride was clearly blinding him from investigating the case clearly. It all sounded really bad, but I didn't mind. All I heard was the one line that Roxy said earlier.

"Did you say that there's a reward out for this Riddle-Man?" I said.

Roxy nodded.

"Yeah. You bet there is. It's a 100, 000 Robux."

"Whoa!"

I almost fainted as I heard the number. A hundred grand! I had never held that much Robux in my life. That was a whole lot of money, and I was flat broke. I thought that I could really use that cash, and they instantly gave me a reason to chase down this Riddle-Man.

"A hundred thousand Robux! That is a whole lot of cash and dinero!"

"You think you can catch him, Noob? I don't mean to burst your bubble or anything, but the whole police department has tried and failed to catch him. No offense, but I can't see how a new guy that wanders into town can do what an entire department can't."

Roxy was right. He wasn't a mean guy like the chief, and I could see that he was just being sincerely doubtful. Yeah, I guess you kinda couldn't blame him. His words did carry a lot of weight. How was I supposed to catch this guy, when the whole Bloxburg police couldn't? It seemed like a fantasy of some kind but I didn't care. All I could think about was that hundred grand Robux. I was tired of being so broke, and I wanted to have that cash. If I had to catch a thousand Riddle-Men, I would do it for that price.

"I don't know, but I'll find some way to do it!"

I heard the chief snicker and chuckle as I spoke. I didn't know what to make of that laugh of his. It was the laugh of a tiger before it pounced on unsuspecting prey. I'm not even sure if tigers know how to laugh, so let's just say that the chief was really intimidating.

"I like your spunk, Noob. Maybe I judged you wrong. Anyone who wants to take down the Riddle-Man is good in my book."

"Uhm, oh-kay."

I didn't know what to make of the chief's comment. Like I said, he sounded like some kind of giant cat on the prowl or something. He was anything but friendly, so I was pretty cautious with him. Hey, can you blame me if I don't trust dudes who just arrested me?

"You want that reward money badly, so it's obvious that you don't have no robux on you."

"I'm flat broke, chief."

"Being flat broke, it doesn't take a detective to know that you've got nowhere to go."

I shrugged my shoulders.

"If you gave me the chance to explain myself earlier, I would have told you that I'm a wandering soul-type of guy. I wander the servers looking for action and adventure. I don't have any permanent home."

"The kind of guy with no permanent address, eh? Don't tell me. Someone framed you for some murder you didn't commit, you're running from the law, and you wouldn't want me to make you angry, right?"

"I don't know what you're talking about, chief."

The chief burst into more laughter and slapped my back so hard, I thought I would puke on the spot. Somehow, I managed to hold in my last meal.

"I'm just kidding with you! That was another wanderer from a long time ago, and somewhere else! Anyway, I digress. We need to catch the Riddle-Man pretty desperately, and I did act a little hasty earlier. Since you don't have a place to stay, I know of the perfect way to make it up to you."

"How is that?"

"You can stay with some of my friends, Ruby and Dylan. They're just as determined to catch the Riddle-Man like yourself, and they always love to entertain guests. You can stay with them, and the three of you can work together and help us catch this Riddle-Man!"

"Whoa, whoa! I haven't even asked permission from them yet. I haven't even met them yet!"

The chief shook his head, and it was clear that he had already made up his mind. There was no arguing with him, and he was already reaching for his office phone.

"I'll call them now. Don't worry about it. Dylan owes me big, and he and Ruby will be more than happy to take you in. They would take you in, even if Dylan didn't owe me. I told you before, they love guests!"

I shrugged my shoulders. I guessed there was no point in arguing with the chief. Besides, who was I to turn down free lodging?

"You don't have to worry about a thing, Noob! Dylan and Ruby are two of the most upstanding citizens of Bloxburg. Believe me, they'll be happy to take you in." Roxy said.

Officer Roxy was a lot more reassuring than the chief. I could see that Roxy was a nice cop, and I couldn't imagine how hard it was to work with the chief.

"I'll take your word for it, Roxy. Can I take a look at the note the Riddle-Man sent?"

"Eager to start already, eh? Well, why not? Good luck trying to solve it though. He always sends us these riddles before he does a crime. It's the perfect way to taunt us, and we've never solved a single one of them!"

I took a look at the paper, and I immediately read the riddle.

Soft, hairy, from door to door. I am the pet that always stays on the floor. What am I?

"Boy that's a tough one. It's usually something that he steals from one of the houses in Bloxburg. I just don't know what that could be." Roxy said.

It did sound tough and baffling. My mind wrestled with the riddle, but not for long. The chief put down the phone and nodded at me.

"I just spoke to Dylan and Ruby. They'll pick you up here in a few minutes." he said.

Chapter Four

Right Under My Nose.

It didn't take me long to settle down in Dylan and Ruby's place. The two of them were nice and friendly enough. What was pretty clear was that the two of them had a definite interest and passion in catching this Riddle-Man of Bloxburg.

"So, you want to catch the Riddle-Man of Bloxburg too, Noob?" Dylan said.

"Yeah. I mean, who wouldn't want to catch that dude? With all that robux they're offering, I could really use the cash."

"Well, tell you what. Me and Dylan will give you an offer you simply can't refuse." Ruby said.

"Try me."

"We'll help you catch the Riddle-Man, and you can even keep all the robux."

"Whoa! That just sounds too good to be true!"

I couldn't believe what Ruby and Dylan were proposing. They both only smiled at me, and I could tell that they were both very serious in their proposal. I simply couldn't believe it. I mean, they had already been very kind to me, giving me a place to stay. Now, they were telling me that they would help me catch the Riddle-Man, and just let me keep all of the robux? Come on, there had to be some kind of catch, right?

"It's true, Noob. There's no catch." Dylan assured me.

"We both just want to catch this guy really badly." Ruby said.

"Okay, pardon me for asking, but why would you do that? I mean, why would you want to catch this guy with no reward for yourselves?" I asked.

Dylan smiled at me.

"Ever heard of Sherlock Holmes, Noob?" he said.

"I'm vaguely familiar with him. He was a great detective who lived in England back in the time of dinosaurs, right?"

Ruby chuckled.

"Close enough."

"He was a famous detective who was aided by his assistant Watson. Together, they solved a lot of crimes that was considered unsolvable back then. He really made a name for himself back then, and his only really tough opponent was a dude named Moriarty. That guy always stretched Sherlock Holmes to the limit. Both of them ended up getting killed in the end."

"Well, that doesn't sound so pleasant." I said.

"Most of the great stories aren't. However, Holmes and Watson were forever immortalized as the greatest detective duo ever."

"Me and Dylan look up to them. We want to be the best detectives that Bloxburg has ever known. This Riddle-Man is our toughest opponent, and we both want to stop him at all costs. The money isn't important to us anymore. You said it yourself. Everyone's got a great home here in Bloxburg. The only important thing now is finding out who the Riddle-Man is, and stopping him."

"We want to be the greatest detectives ever, but we're not above asking for help, Noob. When the chief told us about you, and how you wanted to catch the Riddle-Man, we knew that we could use your help."

"You know the chief personally?" I asked Dylan.

"We were best buds back in the day. He's as law-abiding as we are. He wants to protect Bloxburg just as much as we do."

"I know he can be a bit well, extreme." Ruby said.

"He's just really passionate about his work. That's

why he can kinda go overboard sometimes."

"Tell me about it." I said.

The memory of being chased by the dogs all over town, and being locked up in a cell was still fresh in my mind. I sure didn't want to experience anything like that, anytime soon. However, we were up against the Riddle-Man, and from the way they described him, he would be a really tough opponent. It didn't matter to me, though. What was important for me, was the cash. I really needed all that robux and then some.

"Enough about the chief. Now that we've made our introductions, it's time we all got to work." Dylan said.

He showed me to a large whiteboard. The whiteboard was taped over with several notes and newspaper clippings. There were articles about the Riddle-Man, and some notes like the one that I had read in the precinct, earlier. The whiteboard was taped full of the clippings, and there was no vacant space left.

"This is all the info we've got on the Riddle-Man. We've pored over it over and over again. We've even solved some of the riddles, but the cops didn't listen. Now, they're a lot more receptive."

"You see, the Riddle-Man sends riddles that are really clues to what he's going to steal next. He's literally taunting the police to catch him." Ruby said.

"I can see that this guy has a serious problem with his ego." I said.

"I mean, if you're sending clues like riddles, taunting the cops, you really think you're somebody and anyone else is nobody."

"Serious issues indeed."

"Well, do we have any suspects at least?" I asked.

Both Dylan and Ruby shook their heads.

"No. Bloxburg is a nice little town, with no prior history of anything bad like this. I mean, everybody knows everyone else here." Ruby said.

"Exactly. No one has any idea who would do this. Everybody is everyone else's friend 'round these parts. I don't agree with what my bud the chief did to you Noob, but I know him well enough by now. He did that because he didn't know what else to do. He had no leads, and when the dogs all saw a newbie enter the town well, you know the rest."

Ruby chuckled.

"The chief has his heart in the right place, but he's never been one to check his facts or do some investigating."

"Speaking of investigating, we had better start doing some of our own here. Noob, you got a copy of that latest riddle of Riddle-Man, right? Any ideas?"

It was right then, that it happened. It was like a light

switch was turned on in my head when Dylan asked me that question. I had been thinking of the answer the whole time, on the ride back to their place. Now it hit me. It was so simple, that I didn't know why I didn't think of it sooner. The answer was right under my nose.

"I know the answer!" I said.

Chapter Five

A Thing of Beauty. A Work of Art.

"Soft, hairy, from door to door. I am the pet that always stays on the floor. What am I? I thought it was a dog, at first. Guess I was wrong." Roxy said.

"Use your head, Roxy! A dog doesn't stay on the floor all day! Noob solved the riddle, and tipped us off, but it was way too late. That dastardly Riddle-Man had already struck."

"You can't really blame Roxy, chief." I said.

"The Riddle-Man was banking on that pet thing to throw us all off. The fact is, the answer was never a pet at all. It was a sly play of words."

"Nice thinking Noob. Don't worry. We'll catch this guy. Eventually."

It was the chief in one of his better moods. I had solved the riddle, and we were all huddled together in the house that was burglarized by the Riddle-Man.

Yep. We were all too late.

The house's owner Mr. Blocko was beside himself.

"He took it! He took my precious.."

"We'll get it back. Don't worry, Mr. Blocko." the chief interrupted.

"It's too late! He already took my most prized possession, and you couldn't stop him!"

"Uhm, guys? I don't mean to make things worse, but that's not the only thing that the Riddle-Man did." I said.

"What now, Noob?" the chief said.

"He took Mr. Blocko's prized possession, and he's going to strike again."

I took out a piece of paper from where the Riddle-Man had struck. Everyone was so shocked at what happened, that no one noticed it. I was the only one who saw it.

"What does it say?" Ruby asked eagerly.

"I have a ring, but no fingers. I used to stay still all the time in the past, but now, I follow you around. What am I?"

"Great. Another tough riddle!" the chief said.

He was really getting annoyed with this Riddle-Man. I could see that the chief was stumped, like we all were. Roxy tried to comfort him, but it was no use.

There seemed to be no stopping the Riddle-King!

Everyone seemed quite down and sad by the result of the investigation, but not Dylan. He was already thinking of the answer, and a whole lot more.

"We'll catch this guy. I know it." he said, plainly.

"Why do you say that? He's stumped us so many times already." Roxy said.

"Don't feel down, Roxy. This Riddle-Man wants to get caught. These riddles are some sort of compulsion on his part. He wants to act like he's smart and all, but I can sense that a part of him is actually crying out for help. It's a cry for recognition and attention."

"Smart. Really smart and deep thinking." I said.

"That's Dylan for you. He's always trying to get into the head of any of these perps. This Riddle-Man is really someone complex and Dylan enjoys trying to figure him out." Ruby said.

"There's nothing fun about a burglar taunting the police and stealing stuff from good citizens! We have to figure out where he's going to strike soon!" the chief said desperately.

My mind raced to find the answer to the next baffling riddle. Like all riddles, it was a mishmash of opposite ideas, and it seemed like nonsense. Figuring out riddles was a lot like finding a needle in a haystack, or finding your way in the dark. It seemed so difficult, until you really focused and concentrated on the answer. You also had to keep poking, keep moving, until you found the answer. When the answer was found, all that nonsense always made sense. It was almost like a thing of beauty, or a work of art. The answer always was.

"I figured it out! We have to head to the Roblox Museum of History!" I said.

"So what is he going to steal? A thing of beauty? A work of art?" Roxy asked eagerly.

I nodded with all seriousness.

"This object is kinda both." I said.

Chapter Six

A Blast from the Past and the Next Riddle.

Well, we all raced to the Roblox Museum of History. It was a museum that housed all sorts of artifacts throughout history. A lot of stuff was a blast from the past. We all raced there as fast as we could, but the result was the same.

The Riddle-Man had stolen his artifact. It was pretty old, and could easily fetch a good fortune to collectors or history buffs. The shattered glass display taunted us, just as the riddles taunted the cops. This was getting frustrating.

"No one can move this fast! How could he have stolen it so soon?" the chief said.

"This Riddle-Man is a real menace. It's almost as if he's one step ahead of us all the time." Roxy said.

"Tell me something I don't know. He always IS one step ahead of us. He's making fools of us all." the chief said.

The chief was really starting to lose his patience and for good reason. This Riddle-Man was starting to seem like a force of nature, and not just some common thief. His skills were amazing, and we simply couldn't catch him. It was like playing a futile game of "Catch me if you Can." It was a game we were losing, and we were still playing.

"I don't want you to blow your top any more than you already have chief, but there's another note." I said.

I held up the note, and the chief slapped his forehead in frustration.

"This has to stop somehow!" he said.

"It's a short one. It reads; 'I am black and white and full of fuzz. What am I?' "

The chief raised his hands in frustration, and shook his head.

"No idea! I can't take any more of this!"

"Neither can we. We'll need to think this through in our place. We have to get going. Ruby, Noob, and myself will brainstorm over this at home." Dylan said.

He was also sounding as if he were about to crack. The Riddle-Man was starting to get to us all. I could imagine the Riddle-Man, wherever he was laughing and mocking us all. We all just couldn't catch him, and Bloxburg was suffering for it.

"I don't blame you, Dylan. You guys go back home and think about it. I think we should all take time out and try to figure this perp's method to madness."

"Thanks chief."

Dylan's voice was exhausted, and we all left him him and Roxy in the museum. I actually felt bad leaving them there, staring at the empty and shattered display case. Was there any way to stop this Riddle-Man of Bloxburg?

We all got into Dylan's car, and it was just the three of us. Once we got inside, Dylan's behavior suddenly changed. He wasn't feeling tired anymore, and seemed full of energy again. He smiled at me and Ruby. We both immediately noticed it.

"Whoa, what's up, Dylan? Why are you smiling?"

"Ruby's right. There's no reason to be smiling over anything. The Riddle-Man's got us stumped. We're no closer to catching him, and he's stealing at will now."

Dylan shook his head.

"Maybe not anymore. I think I've figured it all out. I think we can catch the Riddle-Man, but we have to act now."

We drove off.

Chapter Seven

The Riddle-Man Revealed, At Last!

Dylan drove to the police station, as fast as he could. We made it there, before any of the other cops. It was already late at night, and there were only a few cops inside. Most of them were out patrolling Bloxburg. There were a few catching up on office work. Overtime, filling up reports and other boring stuff, I guess. None of them had any idea what was about to happen, and neither did Ruby and I.

We entered the police station easily. They all knew who we were, and they all valued the work that Ruby and Dylan had done for the police. Their investigative work was very much appreciated, and no one questioned why we were there, at that hour.

"What are we doing here?" I asked Dylan.

"We're going to catch the Riddle-Man, Noob. If my hunch is right, he's going to strike at the police station. He's going to steal something here, and it will be the ultimate insult to the cops. If he pulls it off, he will prove without a shadow of a doubt, that he can run rings around the police with little effort."

"Something about his ego, and wanting to be caught, right?" Ruby said.

Dylan nodded.

We made our way down to the storage area of the police. Most of their equipment was there. Sure enough, we caught sight of a shadowy figure walking about. It was just as Dylan had predicted. The Riddle-Man was going to strike in the place everyone least expected him to strike, at the police station.

We cornered the shadowy figure, and I expected to see the Riddle-Man, only we didn't. We saw someone else, and I knew that Dylan was wrong.

"Chief! What are you doing here?" I asked.

"What am I doing here? What are you three doing here? I'm just here checking stuff out. I am the chief of police after all." he said.

The chief spoke calmly and without any kind of fear or tension. Dylan saw him, and he suddenly felt sad and disappointed. He shook his head, and took out a small revolver.

"Give it up, Chief. We already figured it out. There's no need for you to put up a show any more."

"What are you talking about, Dylan? I'm the police chief, for crying out loud! I'm just spending a late night at the precinct, checking things over! Now, put that gun down!"

Dylan shook his head.

"I realized that the only way the Riddle-Man was getting the jump on the police was if he was a cop himself. That way, he could send the riddles, after the crime was done. There would be no way to catch him then. I actually expected it to be Roxy, but I never expected it to be you, Chief."

The chief shook his head. He seemed a lot more nervous now.

"Dylan, I don't know what you're talking about."

"Yes, you do. I can see that slip of paper that's folded in your pocket. That's going to be the next riddle that the Riddle-Man would have left here after you stole that thing from the precinct. The Riddle-Man would have thumbed his nose at the police yet again. Why, Chief? Why?"

It was a brilliant plan, but Dylan had figured it all out. The chief realized that everything was futile now. He raised his hands up in surrender.

"Why, Dylan? Why? You said it yourself. The Riddle-Man wants to insult the police. He wants to insult authority and the law. You always loved the law, Dylan. That's why you wanted to become a great detective. You were becoming famous with your skill and smarts. Me? I've always been the dumb police chief with his heart in the right place. It wasn't fair!

I wanted to be smart and famous like you! The only way to do that was to reinvent myself, to create.."

"..the Riddle-Man. It fits in perfectly." I said.

Ruby was already cuffing the police chief behind him. There was no way he was going to escape now. The reign of the Riddle-Man was finally over.

"I would have pulled it off, if it wasn't for.."

"Wasn't for what, Chief?" Dylan asked.

The chief stopped himself.

"I don't know. I guess you just beat me, Dylan. You were always the smarter one."

We took the chief to the other cops, and they were just as shocked as I was. They never figured out the chief to be the Riddle-Man. Did you figure it out?

If you figured it out, email me at
inforobloxiakid@gmail.com :)

If you enjoyed this book, please leave a review on
Amazon! It would really help me with the series.

Best,

Robloxia Kid

FREE
INSTANT DOWNLOAD

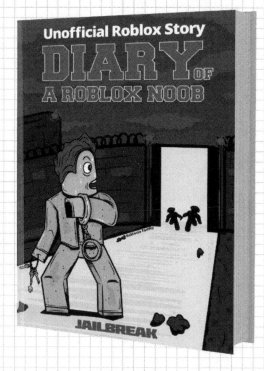

Made in the USA
San Bernardino, CA
16 June 2018